MERCER MAYER'S
LC + THE CRITTER KIDS®

THE
MUMMY'S
CURSE

A Golden Book • New York

Western Publishing Company, Inc., Racine, Wisconsin 53404

A Mercer Mayer Ltd./J. R. Sansevere Book

Library of Congress Catalog Card Number: 93-73739
ISBN: 0-307-15959-0/ISBN: 0-307-65959-3 (lib. bdg.)   MCMXCIV

Written by Erica Farber/J. R. Sansevere

LC

VELVET

LITTLE SISTER

TIGER

KOOL BEAR

SLICK RICK

SU SU GABBY TIMOTHY

GATOR FLEX HENRIETTA

LC and the Critter Kids were going on a field trip to the Critterpolitan Museum.

"Class, I expect you to be on your best behavior today," said Mr. Hogwash.

"Yes, Mr. Hogwash," everyone said, except for LC. He was busy reading a comic book and eating some Chewie Chews.

"Can I have a Chewie Chew?" Gabby asked.

"Here," said LC, taking one out of the box.

"Hey, what comic is that?" asked Gabby.

"*The Curse of the Mummy's Tomb*," answered LC. "Listen to this: 'Whoever opens the mummy's tomb and takes the pendant shall be cursed . . .'"

"That is so dumb," Gabby said.

LC didn't think so. He wondered if the mummy in the museum had a curse on it, too.

LC's class got to the museum early.

"LC, will you take our picture?" Su Su asked.

She and Gabby stood in front of the fountain.

"Okay," said LC. Su Su handed him her camera.

LC clicked it just as two figures walked right in front of him.

"Hey, you messed up our picture!" said Gabby.

"We are sorry, miss," said the shorter critter. "Let's go, Hans."

"But what about the picture?" asked Hans.

"Forget it," said Franz to Hans. "They're just a bunch of kids."

As soon as the museum opened, Mr. Hogwash led the class into the Grand Hallway. "On your right you will see the famous statue of Venus de Gator," said Mr. Hogwash.

"A relative?" asked Henrietta, looking at Gator.

"Beats me," said Gator.

Suddenly something bumped into LC. He knocked into a suit of armor and fell to the floor.

LC looked up as two workmen walked away, carrying a ladder.

"Hey, they're the two guys from the fountain," said LC.

"No, they're not," said Gabby. "They're wearing different clothes."

"It's time to move along to the Egyptian Wing," said Mr. Hogwash.

"I can't wait to see the mummy," LC said to Tiger as they followed Mr. Hogwash down the hall. But when they got to the Egyptian Wing, there was a big rope blocking it off and a sign that said: CLOSED FOR REPAIRS.

"We'll have to see the mummy some other time," said Mr. Hogwash. "Let's move along."

LC looked to the right and then to the left. He just had to see the mummy. It would only take him a minute. No one would ever know. LC slipped under the rope. Then he began to walk slowly toward the tomb.

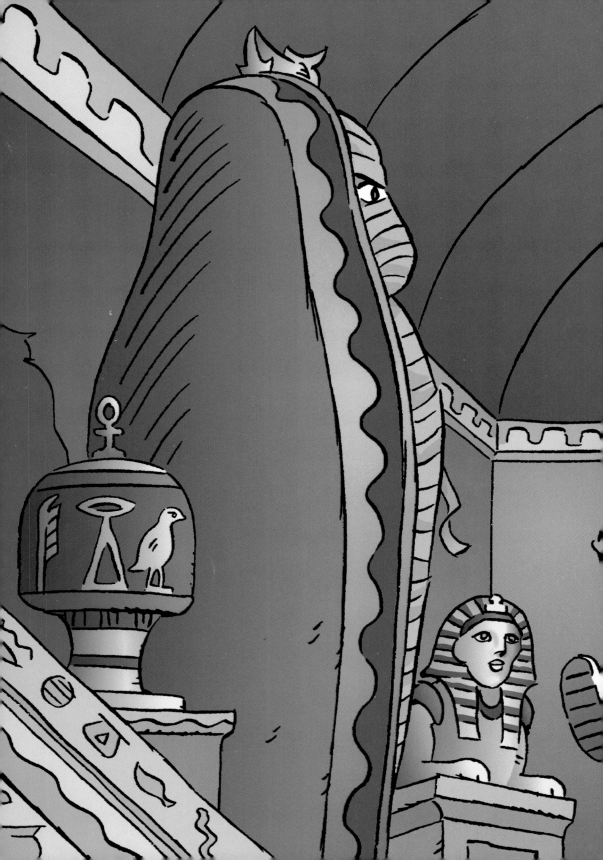

LC crept closer to the tomb. "'Whoever opens the tomb shall be cursed forever . . .'" LC read aloud. So the tomb was cursed, just like the one in his comic. LC backed away.

"Aaaahhhh!!" screamed LC as he backed into someone and dropped his knapsack.

"Aaahhh!" screamed Hans as his knapsack fell to the floor.

LC grabbed one of the knapsacks and dashed out of the room.

Hans picked up the other knapsack.

"Let's look at the pendant," said Hans.

"Not here," said Franz. "Let's go to the bathroom. That way we'll have some privacy."

Hans and Franz snuck out of the Egyptian Wing and slipped into the bathroom.

Hans opened the knapsack. "Chewie Chews," said Hans. "My favorite."

"Chewie Chews?!" said Franz, reaching for the knapsack. "Give me that bag."

Franz dumped everything out of the knapsack. "This is not our bag," said Franz. "It's that kid's. We've got to get our bag back."

"Can I have another Chewie Chew first?" Hans asked. "Please!"

"I'll Chewie Chew you," said Franz. "Now, after that kid. We have no time to lose."

Hans and Franz spotted LC eating lunch.

"There he is," said Franz.

"Where's the knapsack?" asked Hans.

"It's under the table," said Franz. "Go get it."

"Why don't you go get it?" asked Hans. "You're shorter than I am."

"Because I'm the brains," said Franz.

Hans crawled under the table.

"I hate to eat and run," Henrietta said as she shoved two cookies in her mouth. "But I think it's time to go to the museum shop."

Hans reached for the knapsack. At that moment Henrietta stood up. She stepped right onto Hans's hand.

"Hey, LC," said Gabby. "Don't forget your knapsack."

"Thanks," said LC. He bent down to pick it up.

LC and the Critter Kids headed toward the museum shop. Hans and Franz were close behind them.

"Oooh, look at those pyramid rings," said Su Su to Gabby. "They're so pretty."

LC stood staring at a six-foot blow-up mummy.

"What are you doing?" asked Gabby.

"Isn't this cool?" said LC. "It's just like the mummy upstairs."

"How do you know?" asked Gabby. "We didn't see any mummies today."

"I've got to get this," said LC.

"What are you going to do with a blow-up mummy?" asked Gabby.

"Can I help you?" asked the sales critter.

"Yes," said LC. "I'll take one of these."

19

LC was the last one on the school bus. Hans and Franz ran into the parking lot just as the bus door closed behind LC. Hans and Franz jumped into their car.

"After that bus," said Franz.

"Which bus?" asked Hans. The museum parking lot was filled with yellow school buses.

"The one on the left," said Franz.

"Left?" asked Hans.

"Right," said Franz. "Hurry or we'll lose them."

Hans gunned the engine and turned to the right. "I said left," said Franz.

"You just said right," said Hans.

"Just go!" yelled Franz.

That night LC and Little Sister were watching TV. Suddenly there was a news flash:

"Today the famous gold pendant belonging to the Tutan-Critter Mummy disappeared from the Critterpolitan Museum."

"Weren't you there today?" asked Little Sister. "Did you see the mummy?"

"Mummy?" said LC. "What mummy?"

Meanwhile Hans and Franz were parked outside LC's house. They had found his bus and followed him home. They were watching his every move.

"He's bringing the knapsack upstairs," said Franz to Hans.

"What are we going to do now?" asked Hans.

"I've got an idea," said Franz. "Let's go."

Later that night LC was lying in bed asleep. Suddenly a figure moved out of the shadows. It was the mummy. It began walking slowly toward LC's house. Its arms outstretched, the mummy came closer and closer.

24

The mummy crashed through the front door. It walked slowly up the stairs and down the hall. Then the mummy crashed right through the door to LC's bedroom.

"Aaahhhh!" LC screamed.

He bolted up in bed. He looked around his room. There was no mummy anywhere. I guess it was just a dream, thought LC.

The next morning LC was sitting in class. He was trying to forget all about the mummy and the missing pendant.

"Pass your homework to the front of the room," Mr. Hogwash said.

LC opened his knapsack and reached inside. His notebook wasn't there.

"Mr. Critter, where's your homework?" asked Mr. Hogwash.

LC put his hand into the knapsack again. His fingers touched something cold and hard. He pulled it out. "Oh, no," said LC. "The mummy's pendant . . ."

"Since you are so interested in mummies, Mr. Critter," said Mr. Hogwash, "you can write a one-hundred-word essay about them."

Great, thought LC. The mummy's curse has already begun.

Meanwhile, back at their hideaway, Hans and Franz were hard at work. Franz was wrapping bandages around Hans.

"Why do I have to be the mummy?" asked Hans. "Why can't you be the mummy?"

"Because you're bigger," said Franz. "You'll make a much better mummy."

"But what about the real mummy?" asked Hans. "What if he sees me?"

"Don't be ridiculous," said Franz. "There's no such thing as walking mummies."

After school LC called an emergency meeting at the clubhouse. Once the Critter Kids got there, LC locked the door. Then he put the pendant in the middle of the table.

"You know the pendant that's missing from the Critterpolitan Museum?" said LC. "This is it."

"Why did you take it?" asked Gabby.

"I didn't," said LC. "Those two guys at the museum took it. And I wound up with their knapsack by mistake."

"I bet it's a fake," said Gabby.

"No, it's not," said LC. "It's real. And the mummy's coming to get me."

"I think LC may be right," Timothy said. "According to the legend, the pendant must be returned to the mummy's tomb or the mummy will never be at rest."

"That's ridiculous," said Gabby. "All we have to do is take the pendant back to the museum."

Henrietta hurried down the sidewalk toward the clubhouse. She noticed a car parked right in front of LC's house. Sitting in the front seat was a mummy.

"What is this neighborhood coming to?" Henrietta said to herself. Then she knocked on the clubhouse door.

Everyone screamed.

"It's the mummy!" LC whispered.

"Turn off the lights so it won't be able to see us," said Timothy.

LC turned off the light. He and the Critter Kids crawled under the table.

"Hey, anybody here?" Henrietta called.
"I thought we were having a meeting."

"Is that you, Henrietta?" LC asked.

"Yeah," she said. "Let me in."

LC opened the door. "Hurry up," he said.
"There's a mummy out there."

"I know," said Henrietta. "He's sitting in a car
right in front of your house."

LC looked out the clubhouse window. He couldn't believe his eyes. "It looks like the guys from the museum who took my knapsack," said LC. "They must be after the pendant."

"I have the perfect plan," said Gabby. "Follow me, everybody."

LC and the Critter Kids followed Gabby out to LC's driveway.

"Oh, no, here comes the mummy!" screamed Gabby. "Quick, LC," she whispered. "Here's the knapsack. Remember—look scared."

Hans moved slowly up the driveway toward LC. He held his arms straight in front of him.

"I'm so scared," said LC. "The mummy's

coming to get us. Aaaahhhh!!"

Gabby and the Critter Kids screamed.

"Give me my knapsack," said Hans.

"Here," said LC.

Hans took the knapsack and walked back down the driveway.

"See," said Gabby. "I told you it would work. Now for part two of the plan."

On the way back to their hideaway, Hans and Franz changed cars in case they were being followed. Then they stopped at McCritter's.

"You were right," said Hans, eating his burger in one bite. "The kid handed the knapsack right over. Are you going to eat your french fries?"

"Yes, I am," said Franz. "And I'm not sharing with you."

"Let's look at the pendant," said Hans.

Franz opened the knapsack. "Hey," he said. "There's no pendant in here. It's just a rock. You nincompoop! Those kids fooled us."

"I did what you said," said Hans. "It was your idea, you know."

"We've got to get that pendant," said Franz.

The next day was Saturday. LC and the Critter Kids were at the bus stop, on their way to return the pendant to the museum.

LC and Gabby were sitting on a bench with the knapsack between them. They knew that Hans and Franz were right behind them, hiding in a tree. It was all part of the plan.

"Do you have it?" asked Gabby.

"Yep," said LC. He took the blow-up mummy out of his knapsack and handed it to Gabby.

Just then the bus pulled up. LC grabbed the knapsack and got onto the bus with the rest of the Critter Kids.

"Drat!" said Franz. "After them, Hans."

41

As soon as LC and the Critter Kids got to the museum, they split up. LC headed up the stairs to go inside. The Critter Kids hid behind a statue in the parking lot, just as Hans and Franz arrived. Hans and Franz got out of their car and ran up the steps after LC.

LC moved slowly toward the mummy's tomb. He stopped in front of it. He pulled the pendant out of the knapsack.

"I'll take that," a deep voice suddenly said.

LC turned around. It was Hans and Franz. Franz grabbed the pendant out of LC's hand. Then Franz and Hans took off down the stairs.

Meanwhile, back in the parking lot, Tiger was blowing up the mummy. It was only half inflated. "I can't breathe," said Tiger. "You try it, Henrietta."

Henrietta grabbed the mummy and blew as hard as she could. The mummy inflated in a minute.

"Okay, let's do it," said Gabby. She opened the back door to Hans and Franz's car.

They put the blow-up mummy in the backseat and then hid behind another car.

A few minutes later Hans and Franz ran down the museum steps. Then they got into their car.

"Finally, the pendant is ours," said Franz. He started the car and looked in the rearview mirror. "Aaaahh!" he screamed. "The mummy!"

Hans and Franz jumped out of the car.

Hans and Franz ran as fast as they could, with the Critter Kids right behind them. Hans and Franz didn't stop until they ran right into LC.

"You take the pendant," Franz said. He handed it to LC. "We don't want it anymore."

Just then Sergeant Pokey appeared. "All right, the gig is up," Sergeant Pokey said. He put handcuffs on Hans and Franz. "I've had my eye on you two for quite some time."

Sergeant Pokey turned to the Critter Kids. "The Critterpolitan Museum has you kids to thank for recovering the missing pendant," he said. "Now there's only one thing left to do."

LC and the Critter Kids followed Sergeant Pokey back to the Egyptian Wing.

"See, here's the real mummy," said Gabby.

LC hung the pendant around the mummy's neck.

"I told you there was no such thing as walking mummies," said Gabby.

At that moment the mummy moved.

"Hey, did you see that?" said LC.

"What?" asked Gabby.

"Oh, nothing," said LC. The mummy winked at him. "Let's go. I think the mummy's finally at rest."